ALLEN COUNTY PUBLIC LIBRARY

P9-EDX-616

jE
Modell, Frank
Ice Cream Soup

pen marks 3/20

CIRCULATING WITH THE LISTED PROBLEM(S):

pen marks and this page torn 9-12-09
mn

DO NOT REMOVE
CARDS FROM POCKET

Frank Modell

Ice Cream Soup

GREENWILLOW BOOKS, NEW YORK

Another
for Luca

Watercolors and a black pen
were used for the full-color art.
The text type is Times Roman.

Copyright © 1988 by Frank Modell

All rights reserved. No part of this book
may be reproduced or utilized in any form
or by any means, electronic or mechanical,
including photocopying, recording or by
any information storage and retrieval
system, without permission in writing
from the Publisher, Greenwillow Books,
a division of William Morrow & Company, Inc.,
105 Madison Avenue, New York, N.Y. 10016.

Printed in Singapore by Tien Wah Press
First Edition
1 2 3 4 5 6 7 8 9 10

Library of Congress Cataloging-in-Publication Data
Modell, Frank.
Ice cream soup.
Summary: Marvin and Milton decide to give
their own birthday party, but they have
trouble making their cake and ice cream.
[1. Birthdays—Fiction. 2. Parties—Fiction]
I. Title.
PZ7.M714Ic 1988 [E] 87-21097
ISBN 0-688-07770-6
ISBN 0-688-07771-4 (lib. bdg.)

Allen County Public Library
Ft. Wayne, Indiana

No one loved parties more than Marvin and Milton. Especially birthday parties.

But this year Marvin's mother said, "No party."
And Milton's mother said, "Maybe next year."

"A whole year is a long time to wait
for a party," said Milton.

"Maybe somebody's giving us a surprise party
and we don't even know it," said Marvin.
"I doubt it," said Milton.
"The only way we can really be sure of having
a party is to give it ourselves," said Marvin.

"How can we do that?" said
   Milton. "Parties cost money."
"They don't have to," said Marvin.
"I can make the paper hats and bring
   my Pin-the-Tail-on-the-Donkey
   from last year."

"And I have lots of balloons I
could blow up," said Milton.
"We'd better get started if
we're going to do all that and get
the invitations out in time."

Milton went to his house
and blew up his balloons
and wrote lots of invitations.

Marvin went to his house
and made lots of paper hats
and wrote his invitations.

The next day everybody in town

was getting ready for the big party.

"What do we do now?" said Milton.

"First we get started on the cake,"
  said Marvin. "You make the icing."

"Maybe we should have tried making
cookies first," said Milton.
"I think we need some expert advice,"
said Marvin.

"Hello, Marvin," said Mr. Hassenfus.

"What's that mess you have there?"

"That's Milton," said Marvin.

"I mean on the plate," said Mr. Hassenfus.

"That's our birthday cake," said Marvin.

"We want to know what we did wrong."

"What you did wrong," said Mr. Hassenfus,
"was not to get a *Hassenfus* birthday cake."

"What do we do now?" said Milton.
"Start a new cake?"
"There's no time," said Marvin. "We
  have to get started on the ice cream."
"I hope it's not as hard to make as
  birthday cakes," said Milton.

"I think we need
more expert advice,"
said Marvin.

"Hello, Marvin," said Mr. Cleaver.
"What do you have there, soup?"
"No," said Marvin, "it's the ice cream
    for the party."

"It's going to be a very funny party
if you serve soup instead of ice cream,"
said Mr. Cleaver.

"We can't have a party with a caved-in,
    burned birthday cake and soupy ice cream,"
    said Milton.
"Sure we can," said Marvin. "Everyone
    will be having such a good time
    they won't even notice."

"I sure hope so," said Milton.

"Here come all the guests."

"Surprise!" said Mr. Hassenfus.

"This party calls for a real birthday cake."

"And real ice cream, too,"
said Mr. Cleaver. "Happy Birthday!"

"Happy Birthday, Milton."

"Happy Birthday, Marvin."